I0649045

John Pell

Over's Hill

And other Poems

John Pell

Over's Hill
And other Poems

ISBN/EAN: 9783337206352

Printed in Europe, USA, Canada, Australia, Japan

Cover: Foto ©Andreas Hilbeck / pixelio.de

More available books at **www.hansebooks.com**

OVER'S HILL,

A POEM,

AND OTHER POEMS.

AND OTHER POEMS,

BY THE LATE

JOHN PELL, ESQ.

EDITED BY THE REV. T. C. HADDON, LL.B.

WITH A MEMOIR OF THE AUTHOR.

LONDON:

HAMILTON, ADAMS & CO., 33, PATERNOSTER ROW.

GREAT YARMOUTH:
W. D. BURTON, 180, KING STREET.
1863.

TO THE MOST NOBLE

The Marquis of Northampton,

THESE POEMS,

THE PRODUCTIONS OF ONE WHO LONG ENJOYED THE

PATRONAGE OF HIS NOBLE HOUSE,

ARE RESPECTFULLY INSCRIBED,

BY HIS OBLIGED AND OBEDIENT SERVANT,

THE EDITOR.

CONTENTS.

—o—

MEMOIR.

—o—

JOHN PELL, the writer of the Poems to which
this notice is prefixed, spent nearly the whole
of his life in Northamptonshire; having been born
at Guilsborough, in the year 1790, and having died
at Yardley-Hastings, in 1862. His early years were
passed under religious influences of a peculiar nature,
the effect of which is apparent in his writings, and
was so on his character to his latest days. But for
the leaven of the Puritans remaining in him, neither
his life nor his writings would have been what they
were. His parents were of the straitest sect of the
Nonconformists, when nonconformity had more of the
sternness of puritanism than belongs to it at present.

The Baptist denomination, at that period, possessed pastors and preachers whose influence was great and whose memory is still cherished. The preaching of such men as ANDREW FULLER and ROBERT HALL, with others of less note, had established a standard of pulpit eloquence, and produced effects intellectual as well as moral, both elevating and durable. The preaching of those days, indeed, formed a very important part of the mental culture of the congregations that attended upon it. The boyhood of our poet fell in this period, which he always regarded so much in the spirit of a *laudator temporis acti* as to leave him but little sympathy with modern nonconformity.

School education, in those days, was far inferior to what it has since become. If the old grammar schools erred by a too exclusive devotion to grammar and the reading of Latin and Greek authors, the schools of the Dissenters erred also in aiming at the communication of a superficial knowledge of many subjects, involving a feeble, inefficient discipline of juvenile faculties. To discipline of this kind it was his misfortune to be subjected; a misfortune at which, in after life, he often expressed his regret. As a boy, he displayed abilities of a very high order, which were never sufficiently exercised by continued application: his school-days where days of comparative idleness, spent in doing only what he could do with ease. If this portion of his life had been passed in one of the schools where sound scholarship was aimed at and attained, he would, no doubt, have become a distinguished scholar: the editor of his literary remains would probably have had to deal with something of greater importance than a small collection of elegiac and lyric poems. At eleven years old, he was encouraged to write English verse, and praised injudiciously for his success in producing good imitations of bad models. A little later, he was employed in composing essays on deep moral and religious subjects, with similar success in the imitation of what, in those days, passed with many persons for fine writing. Thus was his boyhood unhappily abridged, the due development of his powers checked, by being directed to exercises suited only to a more advanced age, the immediate result being a precocity, incompatible with future greatness.

The medical profession being chosen for him, his medical education was commenced at Wellingborough, under Mr. Peck, continued at Northampton, under the celebrated Dr. Kerr, the elder, and finished in London, by the usual routine of lectures and attendance in hospitals. Throughout his life, his character as a medical practitioner retained the impress of that of his master, Kerr, whose favourite pupil he was, and whom he resembled in the sagacity with which he treated disease, as well as in the little aptitude he possessed at explaining the reasons of his treatment.

Men of far inferior abilities have often risen to fame and fortune in the medical profession. From these results he was effectually debarred by a sensitive shyness of character, under the influence of which, he seemed to go through life contentedly as a village apothecary. To the poor, he was ever most considerate and charitable in the exercise of his profession : the mournful respect with which he was followed to the grave by a crowd of this class of his patients, evinced their sense of the loss of a benefactor. The temperament which disqualified him for becoming a fashionable medical practitioner, prompted him at intervals to the exercise of those powers by which he had acquired fame in his early days: he occasionally indulged in verse; though the quantity which had accumulated is but small, considered as the production of a long life. He had expressed a desire to have these pieces printed before his decease, that they might afterwards be distributed amongst his friends as memorials. This project, left unaccomplished in its proper season, is now, from respect to his wishes, carried into effect, so far as difference of circumstances permits. Of the poems, it is scarcely the province of an editor to offer criticism; he may, however, be allowed to express his conviction that competent judges will think them all worthy of preservation,—that the sentiments they express, and the lessons they teach are everywhere good,—that the writer of them might well congratulate himself on their containing

"No line, which, dying, he would wish to blot,"

that throughout, they indicate the ear, and some other qualities, though not the highest, of a true poet.

OVER'S HILL,

A POEM,

AND OTHER POEMS.

LINES WRITTEN ON OVER'S HILL,
NEAR OLNEY.

—o—

YES, here again I stand, where once I stood,
When early days were friendly to my soul,
In calm communion with the wise and good
Of ages past—till night's dark shadows stole
Around me ; and no voice or sound was heard,
Save of yon river's fall and night's delightful bird.

Again, O river ! do I hear thy voice ;
And thy sweet trillings, melancholy bird,
Who seemest in the gloaming to rejoice.
The twilight deepens, as when first I heard
Your natural music, and your magic strain,
Mingling sad sweetness in my boyish cup of pain.

B

Yet, sound ye not as formerly,—" a change
" Hath come upon the spirit of life's dream ;"
Or, wherefore doth your music sound so strange ?
Ye seem the same, and are but what ye seem ;
'Tis I am altered since my spring-time, when
I was a stranger to the ways and woes of men.

I was a stripling, when upon my ears
First struck your natural melodies ; and now
Strange cares and sorrows, if they brought few tears,
Have left their wasting traces on my brow,
Marks of stern, rugged conflict, that the years
Of th' unconscious schoolboy did not, could not know.

Those chimes play sweetly ! so they did of old ;
But altered comes their sweetness to my heart :
The sun set in a blaze of burning gold ;
But not so joyously did he depart,
As when my young imagination threw,
" Gladness o'er all things, beautiful and new."

Then was there poetry in the wintry blast,
And heaven was in the gentle gales of spring ;
The summer flowers breathed incense as I passed ;
All earth and sky, with angels on the wing
Seemed populous and busy, bringing treasures
Of holy hopes and joys, and virtuous pleasures.

Yet, still I love the works of God to scan,
And drink from Nature's chalice undefiled ;
But when the boy ascendeth into man,
He cannot feel as when he was a child,
Standing upon this green hill's beauteous brow,
And listening to the valley's sweet sounds from below.

No more, vain self! no longer here intrude :
Be my soul harmonized to solemn thought ;
Fly all vain passions from this solitude ;
For ages past before my mind are brought,
Ages whose unrecorded deeds have passed away,
Whose every trace and mark have perished in decay.

Yet, sound ye not as formerly,—" a change
" Hath come upon the spirit of life's dream ;"
Or, wherefore doth your music sound so strange ?
Ye seem the same, and are but what ye seem ;
'Tis I am altered since my spring-time, when
I was a stranger to the ways and woes of men.

I was a stripling, when upon my ears
First struck your natural melodies ; and now
Strange cares and sorrows, if they brought few tears,
Have left their wasting traces on my brow,
Marks of stern, rugged conflict, that the years
Of th' unconscious schoolboy did not, could not know.

Those chimes play sweetly ! so they did of old ;
But altered comes their sweetness to my heart :
The sun set in a blaze of burning gold ;
But not so joyously did he depart,
As when my young imagination threw,
" Gladness o'er all things, beautiful and new."

Then was there poetry in the wintry blast,
And heaven was in the gentle gales of spring ;
The summer flowers breathed incense as I passed ;
All earth and sky, with angels on the wing
Seemed populous and busy, bringing treasures
Of holy hopes and joys, and virtuous pleasures.

Yet, still I love the works of God to scan,
And drink from Nature's chalice undefiled ;
But when the boy ascendeth into man,
He cannot feel as when he was a child,
Standing upon this green hill's beauteous brow,
And listening to the valley's sweet sounds from below.

No more, vain self ! no longer here intrude :
Be my soul harmonized to solemn thought ;
Fly all vain passions from this solitude ;
For ages past before my mind are brought,
Ages whose unrecorded deeds have passed away,
Whose every trace and mark have perished in decay.

LINES WRITTEN ON VISITING THE BURIAL PLACE OF THE LATE MARCHIONESS OF NORTHAMPTON.

—o—

I sought the sacred dwelling of the dead ;
   Hushed was all sound of voice, or footstep rude ,
Mem'ries alone of souls from earth long fled
   Were with me, in that ancient solitude ;
Th' escutcheoned wall and monumental urn,
   Recording stories of forgotten woe,
"Of joys departed, never to return,"
   The mourners, with their dead together laid below.

From these I turn—and yon inscription read,
   Which tells of one who met the common doom,
Yet asking more than sorrow's wonted meed—
   Pensive I gaze on epitaph and tomb.

So richly gifted, beautiful and young,
    Earth's richest splendours seemed but meet for thee:
Now thou art dust, and mute the tuneful tongue ;
    Thus all the good, thus all the great shall be.

To him, the widowed partner of her state,
    O'er whom her life its joyous pleasance flung,
Rapt into anguish at her sudden fate,
    His peace all shattered, and his powers unstrung,
O, heartless Death ! for thy remorseless spoil,
    What rank, or wealth, or genius can atone,
Or honours, or all fruits of human toil,
    Since the high mind can love but one alone ?

Pale, sculptured effigy of life in death,
    Well hath a hand, most cunning, traced thy form ;
The speaking lips unstirred by human breath,
    The brow serene, unmoved by passion's storm.
Genius once sparkled in those beamless eyes,
    And triumphed in each moveless feature there :
But who shall rouse them from their cold disguise ?
    What wake to life those lineaments so fair ?

To the dim shelter of this hallowed dome,
    Shall Mercy mild and Pity oft repair,
To gaze delighted on the art of Rome,
    And learn the heart's best, purest lessons there.
That Charity, more during palms bestows
    Than kings and conquerors, in their proudest fane,
Ever had bound upon their laurel'd brows,
    In memory of their triumphs false and vain.

For virtue liveth, after perished art
    Even from remembrance moulders into dust,
The eternal record never shall depart,—
    Whilst urns and vases, faithless to their trust,
With goodly temples, which those treasures graced,
    Become the ruins of a desolate land,
That record in a nobler temple placed,
    Defies all ruin, and shall ever stand.

THE BIRTHDAY.

—o—

Thus nineteen years have passed away,
Since dawned in light thy natal day.
How many more may onward roll,
Ere thou shalt reach life's destined goal,
Or what the colour of thy fate,
A cloudless sun to gild thy state,
Or tempests bursting o'er thy head,
To strike thy dearest comforts dead,
Or sunlit sky dispelling gloom,
To light thee to an honoured tomb—
Which, it imports us not to know :
Enough, that God is good and wise—
Good, if these blessings He bestow ;
Good, when these blessings He denies.
Yes, years roll on—life ebbs apace,
This world is not our resting place :

Its fleetness is the poet's theme,
Its glory but the hero's dream.
'Tis but as yesterday, thy nest
Thou madest on thy mother's breast,
A thoughtless infant; and e'en now,
Woman is written on thy brow.
A change hath passed upon thy lot,
The dreams of infancy forgot ;
Its joys and sorrows all are flown,
As to a world of thought unknown.
Thou hast no memory of the past,
No knowledge of what once thou wast :
When hardly conscious of alarms,
Thou revel'dst in thy mother's arms.
Let not such treasures thriftless pass,
Like sand-grains from th' unheeded glass,
For different far, must be the scene
Unfolded by the next nineteen.
The spirit's joyous bloom must fade,
Life's gorgeous tints no more displayed ;
Thy womanhood the robes shall wear
Of soberness—perhaps of care.

Yet grieve not, nor anticipate
The trials of disastrous fate ;
For though thy sky may darkened be,
And rough thy voyage across the sea,
On the good Pilot place thy trust,
He will secure thy precious dust,
Where care and sorrow are unknown,
The shadow of the Eternal Throne.

LINES WRITTEN IN A LADY'S COPY OF THE MEMOIRS OF HENRY MARTYN.

—o—

'Tis not by length of years
　　We measure life;
Nor by loud groans and tears,
　　The inward strife
　　Of the heart's woe.
The long life oft is brief,
And that the bitterest grief,
　　Where no tears flow.

Man doth not easiest die
　　On silken bed,
With gilded canopy
　　Above his head,

Mocking at death :
The good man heedeth not
Whether in hall or cot,
    He yields his breath.

He liveth long who leads
    A life of prayer ;
And finds, whate'er he needs,
    God everywhere :
'Mid Zembla's ices drear,
Or scorched by Tropic sun,
Breathing, " Thy will be done"—
    Dies without fear.

For thee, I ask no meed
    Of splendid fate ;
Tho destiny's decreed
    Of all thy state,
    Wane and increase ;
But making God thy friend,
Close by a peaceful end,
    A life of peace.

THE TRANSFIGURATION.

(WRITTEN FOR A LADY'S ALBUM.)

—o—

* * * * * * Not in the splendid fane,
Where priests and levites worshipped, and the vain
Children of Mammon sought their sins to hide ;
But Thou didst climb the mountain's desolate side :
Three favoured ones, companions of Thy way,
To witness to Thy glory and to pray.

As awful there, the Man of Sorrows stood,
Lo ! splendours poured upon Him as a flood ;
O'er all His frame the 'luring glories spread,
Gild His meek form and light His reverend head.

And with Him in divine communion stand,
Two elder brothers of that prophet band,
That through long ages had foretold His birth,
And blessed advent to this ruined earth.
Now speak they of the death that He must die;
The last faint beams of his benignant eye,
The cross, the thorny crown, the Roman spears,
His country's taunts and curses; and the tears
Of Mary, mother, blessed more than they,
Who bring to life mere human things of clay.

Dazzled, bewildered by the sacred blaze,
The three disciples tremble as they gaze:
Their transient slumbers pass, as by a word,
And they behold the glory of the Lord!
Then spake the lion-hearted Peter :—" Here
" Let us our tabernacles build; no fear
" Of earthly sorrow shall our spirits wound,
" No sickness vex us, and no griefs confound :
" Placid and calm, as at some silver spring,
" A gentle dove re-plumes her wearied wing;
" So we, apart from earth and earth's employ,
" May spend our holy lives in perfect joy."

Thus Peter spake, in fancied vigour strong,
As the proud steed to battle bounds along,
His breast dilated with unwonted force,
Untired and fearless, rushing on his course.

And didst thou, Peter, on that raptured day,
Dream, on that mount thou couldst for ever stay?
Did no kind angel whisper in thine ear,
Of perjured vows, and honour lost in fear;
No crowings of that ominous bird that spoke
Of forfeit bonds and resolutions broke?

Learn, gentle Maiden, from this record true,
Hourly, by grace, thy virtue to renew—
That human strength, unholpen, is but dust:
Weak all our powers, and vain our firmest trust.

COWPER'S OAK.

—o—

AND art thou still existent, still a tree?
Still rave the wild winds round thine aged head?
While he who sweetly sang, and gave to thee,
A second youth and immortality,
Feels not nor hears them in his narrow bed,
The lonely silent mansion of the dead.

Ages and centuries have passed since thou
Did'st spring a tender sapling from the earth;
Ages passed by, nor left upon thy brow,
Marks save of strength and beauty: even now
Ages may pass, ere prostrate on the earth
Relentless Time may lay thine honours low.

Who planted thee, old patriarch of the wood,
Watch'd thy slow growth, and trained thine infant age,
And haply oft in solemn musings stood,
Scanning the mysteries of thy future page
Of changeful destiny—the ill or good—
By lightning riven, or buoyant o'er the flood?

Hast thou a spirit?   Give it then a voice;
Speak, as of old the mystic Druid spoke,
Who bade a people sorrow or rejoice,
In hollow accents from the sacred oak:
Tell of the horrors of thy youthful time,
The age of feudal violence and crime.

For they were days of violence and blood,
That witnessed the uprising of thy form,
Ere Time had crowned thee monarch of the wood,
Or bowed thy topmost branches to the storm;
And now thy many trials all withstood,
Thou stand'st a silent preacher to the good.

What, silent still! No thrilling tale of blood,
Or lawless violence, or wanton power;
Did guilty footsteps never dare intrude,
Upon thy peaceful, dreamless solitude,
To wake to tears the pity of the good,
And rack the guilty in his dying hour?

Did never thy huge, guilty arms sustain,
The serf that battled by the oppressor's side,
And at the will of that proud master died,
Quivering in agonies of mortal pain?
Tell if thou can'st, if thou can'st find a tongue;
Confirm what tales have told, and elder bards have
    sung.

Where lie the victims of barbarian lust,
And which the hillocks populous with death?
Point to the grey-haired, murdered parent's dust,
Where the lone traveller sighed his latest breath:
Can'st thou not tell the secrets of their tomb,
Nor light the grave's impenetrable gloom?

Stern gnarled chronicler! is there no string
In thy tough heart, that I may touch, no song
Or tale of eld, or of the elfin ring,
No chord to jar thy rugged nerves along,
No midnight legend of the fairy knoll,
To wake the memory of thy slumbering soul?

Did'st never converse hold with Milton—He
The sightless poet of the angelic sphere,
When the dread pestilence of that fatal year,
Bade him to thy contiguous refuge flee,
Had'st thou no knowledge of the illustrious dead,
Or is thy consciousness and memory fled?

Thou speak'st not even of him who sung of thee,
Ungrateful! thou art voiceless in his praise,
Even his whose sweetly melancholy lays
Crowned thine old head with immortality:
Hold'st thou no precious relics of his song,
To whom thy name, and fame, and praise belong?

Old tree, farewell! the fatal hour makes haste,
Shall bring thy faded honours to their tomb,
Nor Cowper's lays, nor Compton's* generous taste,
Can save thee from the inevitable doom:
Even now thy living branches seem to mock
Thy dead and dying members, which the shock
Of the elements hath wasted,—like a wreath
Of summer flowers upon the brow of death.

* The Márquis of Northampton had a board placed on the tree, with an inscription requesting visitors not to mutilate it.

THE VICTIM OF CONSUMPTION.

I saw her in the morn of hope, in youth's delicious
spring,
Elate and joyous as the lark just bursting on the
wing,
A radiant creature of the earth as first it soars on
high,
Without a shadow on its path, or cloud upon its
sky.

I see her yet—so fancy deems—her dark and waving
hair,
Gleaming like shadows upon snow, above her fore-
head fair,
Her large dark eye of glancing light, the winning
smile that play'd
In dimpling sweetness round the mouth Expression's
self had made.

I marked the first faint emblems of Consumption's
hectic wreath,

The boding smiles that spoke to me of treachery
beneath,

Her wasting slenderness of form, her changed yet
lustrous eye.

And sadly said my heart, "O God! and must this
fair one die?"

And long she lingered ere the chain that bound her
spirit broke,

And long and sorely suffered, ere the last resistless
stroke,

That took away all mortal pain and weakness and
disguise,

And her soul upborne upon the wings of angels
sought the skies.

Yet peaceful was its parting from its wasted tene-
ment,

And much of Heavenly mercy with the painful judg-
ment blent,

And blessed airs from Paradise came wafted through
     the gloom,
To cheer and to support her in her passage to the
     tomb.

And now her tenantless remains are decaying in the
     grave,
And above that narrow dwelling doth the grass
     unchidden wave,
Yet again shall life and beauty re-animate her clay ;
For "the sting of death is sin"; and that her Saviour
     took away.

THE PASTOR'S FUNERAL.

—o—

Rapt into anguish at thy sudden doom,
Thy sorrowing people gather round thy tomb,
To pay the last sepulchral honours bend,
And mourn the saint, the pastor and the friend.

No vain display, no mockery of woe,
No laboured art to teach our tears to flow,
No mimic grief nor overacted part;
We mourn thee, with the mourning of the heart.

We mourn the pastor, faithful to his trust,
Whose narrow grave receives his honoured dust :
Widows and orphans drop the gushing tear,
And cry " Our parent, friend, lies buried here."

No gorgeous obsequies thy bones await,
No gilded shrine, nor canopy of state,
Nor blazoned shield suspended o'er thy tomb,
No choral dirge, deepening the midnight gloom.

To their last home, midst gentle mourning strains
In simple state, we've borne thy loved remains,
To rest in friendship with their kindred clay,
Till the last trumpet wake " the rising-day."

Here shall affection, to thy memory true,
This simple grave with plenteous tears bedew,
And lowly bending o'er the unconscious earth,
Embalm the virtues of the Man of Worth.

And O ! if spirits freed from mortal care,
E'er unseen wander through the yielding air,
If, at their will celestial forms can rove,
O'er earthly scenes of labour or of love :—
Here, in this house, the witness of thy prayers,
Scene of thy earnest labours and thy cares,

Where now in slumber rests thy mortal part,
Descend and cheer and animate each heart :
Teach us the alluring charms of sin to fly,
In faith to live, in humble hope to die ;
Our faith confirm, our grovelling thoughts refine,
And raise our fainting powers to bliss like thine.
Whilst on the narrow grave where Whitehead sleeps,
Each pensive mourner bends his eye and weeps,
And busy memory counts his virtues o'er,
And 'wails the friend and shepherd, now no more ;
Let us not mourn as those of hope bereft,
But duteous tread the path our prophet left ;
To his new home let all our wishes rise,
And humbly trace his footsteps to the skies ;
Still keep his bright example full in view,
Nor be this parting scene a last adieu.

LINES ON THE SUDDEN DEATH OF THE REV. HENRY GAUNTLETT, VICAR OF OLNEY.

—o—

Softly, alone and suddenly he passed :
   Even as pale meteors vanish from the night.
So disappeared he from life's dreary waste,
   To rise a bright star in etherial light.
No lingering in his passage, no delay,
   No wearisome anticipated doom,
The summons comes, he speeds him on his way
   One easy step, and he is safe at home.

When princes perish in the battle fray,
   Deep music fills the air, with plaintive strains,
And the proud banner o'er the mangled clay,
   Shields from the common eye the loved remains ;

But thou, dead soldier of the holy cross,
  For thee no nation lifts the funeral wail,
Yet pious spirits weep thy sudden loss,
  And filial mourners turn with sorrow pale.

Frailties had'st thou ?   Thou hast no frailties now,
  Gently thy passions move in sweet accord,
And heavenly splendours clothe that sainted brow,
  Shed from the glory of thy martyred Lord.
Reflected from His God-like face, the rays
  Of light celestial sparkle from the throne;
Thou dost behold His image, and the blaze
  Transforms thee to the likeness of His own.

A glorious change hath passed across the scene
  Of thy o'erlaboured and protracted life :
The great realities then dimly seen,
  Down the dark vista of a world at strife;
Even the deep mysteries of redeeming love
  All stand revealed and open to thine eyes :
To holy joy, thy powers, made perfect, move,
  And glows the enfranchised soul with glad surprise.

Thy "Visions of the Apocalypse,"* are o'er :
   Thou dwellest not dim shadowy forms among ;
With him of Patmos does thy spirit soar,
   Swift as an eagle, as a seraph strong.
Yet wilt thou not on this dark spot of earth,
   Oft turn the glances of that heavenly eye,
To alarm the vicious, check the sons of mirth,
   And teach the suffering Christian how to die?

   * Mr. Gauntlett was the author of a work on the "Apocalypse."

COWPER.

—o—

Thou wast a Christian Poet, and thy muse,
Was fed by other than Castalian dews,
Pure from the rock the stream celestial broke,
And gushed in numbers at the Spirit's stroke ;
O, had thy Homer known a fount like thine !
Then had his numbers been indeed divine.

Thou wast the bard of Liberty ! thy pen
Wrote her best doctrines for thy fellow men ;
Her sacred precepts well adorn thy page,
And bid us scorn the bondsman's heritage ;
And nobly is the lesson taught by thee,—
" He is the freeman whom the truth makes free."

And thou wast Nature's Poet, and didst sing
Of trees and times, and seasons and did'st fling
Even o'er old Winter's cheek of frost and snow,
A mask of lusty beauty and a glow ;
And sweetly didst thou sing of sylvan age,
And well record its lessons in thy page.

And thou wast man, of gentle woman born,
And nought of human could'st regard with scorn :
Whate'er his country, barbarous or refined,
Thou wast his friend and friendly to his kind,
For Jesus' sake thou lovedst him, as He
Once came from heaven and died for love of thee.

Yet thou wast miserable !—on the brink
Of hell thy fancy hovered—thou didst drink
A cup of loathly mingling, even a bowl
Of poisonous mixture—hemlock to thy soul :
Midst clouds thy sun sank into trackless night,
And left thee with thy God, without one ray of light.

BURNS AND HIS FRIENDS.

-—()—-

" O! WILLIE brewed a peck o' maut,
  " And Rob and Allan cam' to prie,
" Three blither hearts, that lee-lang night,
  " Ye wadna' find in Christendie.

CHORUS.

  " We are no' fou, we're na' that fou,
    " But jist a drappie in our ee',
  ·" The cock may craw, the day may daw',
    " But aye we'll taste the barley bree."

Sae Willie, Rob, and Allan sang,—
  Sae taunted Time wi' wit and glee ;
And, aye, the chorus, all night lang,
  Was, as we're now, we hope to be—

" For we're no' fou, we're na' that fou,
  " But jist a wee drap in our ee'
" The cock may craw, the day may daw';
  " But still we'll taste the barley bree."

Time heard their taunts and gript his scythe,
  And sware an aith, they weel might dree,
Had they dreed aught, while bold an' blithe,
  They sang inspired wi' barley bree:
" We are na' fou, we're na' that fou,
  " But jist a drappie in our ee'.
" The cock may craw, the day may daw',
  " But aye we'll taste the barley bree."

He sware, short while the cock should craw,
  Their harbinger of morn to be;
For them, short time, the day should daw',
  Wi' golden tint on tower and tree:
Short while, for them, the moon's pale horn
  Should gild the scene o'er land and lea,
Ere hapless dawned the fatal morn
  Should gild the graves of all the three.

And soon, too soon, his aith was proved,
    Though in its proof, sma' pairt had he,
Their death was from the life they loved,
    Their mortal drap, the barley bree.
Nae mair they'll sing,—" We're no' that fou;"
    Nae mair the drap be i' their ee',
Nor cock shall craw, nor day shall daw'
    For them, while o'er the barley bree.

Soon Learning mourned for Willie gane,
    For Robin, Poesy wet her ee',
And Science made for Allan mane,
    Sin' Death's dark house held all the three.—
Britons! lament for genius rare,
    All victims of the barley bree,
And ban the bree, that would na' spare
    The precious lives o' sic a three.

LINES ON AN INCIDENT OF THE PENINSULAR WAR.*

—o—

Blow, fiercely blow thou bitter blast,
  Lightning and thunders rend the skies;
And bid thy waves, thou ocean vast,
  In horriblest confusion rise:
Let the wild land-storm pour its rages,
  And sweep a nation to the tomb;
Fling ruin o'er the boast of ages,—
  It is His hand that writes their doom.

But deadlier far, the awful scene,
  The horrors of that fatal day,
When rival ranks of dauntless mien
  Perished amid the mortal fray.

* The death of a young Subaltern, which was attributed to fatigue and
exhaustion.

O ! faithful to their country's trust,
    But few, alas! remained to tell
How many a hero to the dust,
    'Mid prayers and shouts, and curses fell.

Fought is the battle, and 'tis won,
And the day's work of death is done.
The veteran, leaning on his spear,
Scarce can repress the bitter tear,
As wildly, and with faltering breath,
He views the awful scene of death :
How many a kind and early friend,
This day hath reached his journey's end!

Sad musings stealing o'er his mind,
He weighs the madness of mankind :
Around lie slaughtered foes and friends ;
With life their awful variance ends :
Foeman and friend resign their breath,
In the still fellowship of death.

Deep-whelmed beneath the human wave,
A host of heroes found their grave;
Upon their common parent's breast
Bravely they fought, and sunk to rest.
But whose that pale, that bloodless mien,
Strange contrast with this gory scene?

Unbruised amid this human storm,
No scars deface his youthful form,
Faint and exhausted, on the ground,
And dying, yet without a wound!
Say, is it Death has closed his eyes,
Or is it aught in Death's disguise?
He breathes yet;—ere the night-dew falls,
Bear him to yonder convent walls,
Let holy sisters round his bed,
The pious dews of mercy shed;
Their kindly bosoms ever glow,
At sight of suffering and woe;
They best invite returning sense,—
Then comrades, softly, bear him hence.

Safe from this scene of war's alarms,
They bore him up in soldiers' arms :
And holy sisters on his head,
The dews of pious mercy shed,
And wept and prayed, and gently strove
To show a mother's, sister's love,
And kindly tended by his side,
Till in their gentle arms he died.

His death no stone records—his birth,
His name, his lineage, or his worth :
They laid him in a rural tomb,
Deep hidden in umbrageous gloom.
And there as sweetly doth he rest,
With foreign soil above his breast,
As though his tenantless remains,
Mouldered beneath his native plains.

Avails it how we yield our breath,
Or where we meet the stroke of death,

Whether in shades of night we die,
Or in the day's most busy eye,
Alone, or in the midst of friends,
This feverish dream of being ends?

Companion of those genial hours,
When pleasure strewed our path with flowers,
Adieu! thy voyage of life is o'er,
Thou'rt stranded on a foreign shore:
Thine was the soul of honour, thine
The heart that bowed at pity's shrine.
No braver trod the path of blood,
No gentler roamed the village wood:
Adieu, thy pilgrimage is o'er,
Ended upon a friendly shore.

THE DYING POLE.

—o—

BEAR up, bear up, a little while, as yet my throbbing
heart,
  O close not yet, on all I love, my dim, my closing
  eye ;
Too true, ye tell me, and I feel that I must soon
depart ;
  Yet for my dear, my native land 'tis comely thus
  to die.
The sun is sinking in the west, his daily race is
o'er,
Mine too is sinking, and shall rise, ah! never, never
more.

Thy blessed beams, O Sun, no more shall wake me
in the morn ;
  For me no more the merry lark shall heavenward
  soar and sing ;

No more for me the silver moon shall lift her stately
    horn,
  Nor round my homeward evening path her quiet
    radiance fling :
From this cold earth, my colder limbs shall never
    more arise,
And I no more shall watch you as ye triumph
    through the skies.

Beyond those swelling mountains, now tinged with
    evening light,
  I lived my mother's darling and my father's
    chiefest joy,
O! could they now behold me, and bless my failing
    sight,
  'Twould be a comfort to their hearts to tend their
    dying boy :
How tenderly they'd look on me and catch my part-
    ing groan,
Ah me! there is no hope of this; and I must die
    alone.

Alone! no, God is with me, and His arm sustains my
 head,
He never can abandon the spirit of the free,
And while I'm shivering into death upon this grassy
 bed,
His blessed saints and angels shall tend and com-
 fort me :
Pro me orate! Blessed Saints, a slain, a dying boy,
And guide me where the bond is free, nor tyrants
 can destroy.

'Tis well nigh over—my fixt eye no object can discern;
To Thee, O God of Liberty, my breaking heart I turn;
Look on me where I lie ; accept a Polish patriot's
 blood ;
Make it a stream of life and strength, that, as a
 mighty flood,
Shall drown oppression, and destroy the counsels of
 the wise,
And teach the proud and merciless, their refuges are
 lies.

LINES ON THE DEATH OF THE REV. JOHN SEAGRAVE, RECTOR OF CASTLE ASHBY.

TOLL the mournful passing bell,
Sound the deep funereal knell!
A mortal hath escaped from earth,
Achieved the object of his birth,
Eternity's dark veil hath riven,
And changed this earthly scene for heaven.

Mourn, ye who knew and loved him, mourn;
To you he never shall return:
His well-accustomed step no more,
Shall meet you at the cottage door,
No more his lips good counsel give,
To teach its inmates how to live,

The good to praise, the evil warn,
To cheer the suffering and forlorn,
Or point his flock to wisdom's way,
Or teach the infant mind to pray.

Mourn, ye who knew and loved him, mourn;
To you he never shall return,
His willing hands no more dispense,
The alms of kind beneficence,
His feet no more the pathway tread,
That to the abodes of sickness led;
The beauteous scenes so often trod,
The churchward path, the pleasant sod,
Those feet shall mutely mark no more;
Their mortal pilgrimage is o'er.

Mourn, ye who knew and loved him, mourn;
To you he never may return:
That solemn brow, thought's favorite spot,
Its musings all are quite forgot:
That ear which drank the tale of grief,
To you is now for ever deaf:

The manly heart, life's business o'er,
Its steady pulses beat no more,
The worn-out frame of reverend grace,
Hath found its last fit resting-place.

Nay, mourn not, ye who loved him here,
Or, shed but memory's placid tear;
Life's mouldering organs do but sleep;
But he hath passed the stormy deep,
The fabled stygian stream hath passed
And reached his final home at last.
The dream is o'er, the feverish strife,
And death is swallowed up of life.

NOVEMBER REFLECTIONS.

—o—

DARK is the morn, and through the air
  The spirit of the tempest flies,
Nature, of late, so bright and fair,
  Adorned with flowers of thousand dyes,
    All beauteous to the view,
Now shrinking from the tyrant blast,
Appears a desolated waste,
And reads this lesson to the mind—
Such is the fate of human kind,—
    A lesson sad yet true.

The voice of melody that late,
  Re-echoed through the listening grove;
Hath it, alas! so short a date,
    Is all on which we fix our love,
      So perishing and frail?
'Tis but as yesterday, the scene,
In varied robes of cheerful green,
From early morn to closing day,
Looked rich and beautiful and gay,
      And told a lovelier tale.

November comes, and at his call,
  The genius of the storm awakes,
Flowers fade—the leaves deciduous fall,
    The vision flies, the enchantment breaks,
      And vanishes away.
Now drenched with cold and cheerless rains,
  The shepherd tends his fleecy care,
And wet-shod traverses the plains,
    Erewhile with summer beauty fair;
In his dull eye and aching breast,—
In all, this moral stands confest—
      Life is no summer's day.

Yet are there some, whose feelings beat
    Responsive to the fading year,
Who tread with pleased and willing feet,
    The leafless grove, the pathway drear,
      Nor converse hold with joy;
Who hail dread winter's darkest gloom,
    Nor fear a rougher path;
Who welcome Fate's severest doom,
    Welcome the bed of death:
O'er whose bared heads, the storm hath passed
Alone on life's bewildered waste;
Who bare their bosoms to the blast
    And bid its rage destroy.

Is there an outcast tempest-driven,
    Tossing on life's uncertain sea,
No home on earth, no hold on heaven?
    Poor wretch! who would not pity thee?
For thee no happier day shall dawn,
    No kind and cloudless skies,
Nor glory's pure perpetual morn,
    Awake thy ravished eyes.

E

The wint'ry storm shall pass away,
    The tempest cease its horrid strife,
The summer sun prolong the day,
    Re-quickening Nature into life;
But Man shall wither as the grass,
    Youth, health and beauty quickly fade,
Wealth, pride and pomp as quickly pass,
    Low in the dust together laid.

EVENING AFTER A BATTLE.

——o——

FOUGHT is the battle and 'tis won,
And the day's work of Death is done:
Down in the west the sun is sinking,
   Gilding the hills with lingering light,
And from sad scenes of horror shrinking,
   Bids a conflicting world, good night.

Fair was thy rising, glorious sun,
   Unlike a harbinger of sorrow,
'Mid clouds thy noon-tide race was run,
   But thou shalt rise as fair, to-morrow,

                  E 2

And in contempt of human strife,
   Thou shalt repair thy wasted beams,
And fling o'er every haunt of life,
   In gorgeous pomp, thy golden gleams.

Fair was thy rising; thy first rays
   Shed gladness o'er the western mountains;
Nought but the matin song of praise,
   The tuneful groves and bubbling fountains,
Disturbed the silence of the scene:
'Twas calm and quiet and serene.
Morning her glories o'er the landscape threw,
Green as the spring, and glittering with dew.

But whence that wild continuous blast,
   That roar which filled the swollen gale,
As late with heavy gust it passed
   And mountain echoes sped the tale?
It was the awful voice of War;
   Carnage and Death were in his train,
Behind his desolating car,
   Were Horror, Famine, Grief and Pain.

I cannot paint the mortal strife,
  The shrieks, the groans, the dying anguish :
Such awful waste of human life
  Would make the fiercest spirit languish.
The deep-mouthed clarion's warlike tones,
Mix with the dying soldier's groans,
As fainting on the earth he lies,
And feebly shouting "Victory!" dies.

HENRY MARTYN.

—·—

In climes remote, where moral death
    O'er all with horror frowned,
And Error with contagious breath
    Spread pestilence around.

No friendly hand was there, to close
    His dim and wearied eyes,
But bowed by solitary woes,
    The Christian pilgrim dies.

Yet there, how sweetly doth he rest,
    In Tocat's burning sands,
With foreign soil above his head,
    Entombed by stranger hands.

Joyful from that lone desert shrine,
   His sacred dust shall rise,
By angel summons called to join
   His Saviour in the skies.

IN MEMORY OF WILLIAM DE NORMANN.

—◦—

It was not in the battle, it was not in the storm,
No bullet pierced his bosom, no lightning scathed his
      form,
Nor wasting Tropical disease, nor fever's parching
      breath
Crushed his young life and living hopes into the
      house of Death.

    Faultless in person, with a noble mind,
    In manners courteous, manly yet refined,
    Aye true to conscience and to duty's call,
    To friends his love, and honour due, to all:
    These could not save from treachery accurst;
    By torture wasted, the strained heart-strings burst:

And, hope and life expiring, prone he fell,
'Mid perjured fiends, foul ministers of hell.
Bury the dead! though in a borrowed grave;
And deeply mourn, though impotent to save.
Yes, bury him in that sequestered spot:
The cords are broke, the agony forgot.
He sleeps in peace: the immortal ends not here,
He waits his summons to a brighter sphere.
A body lies near Pekin's gorgeous towers,
But he has rest;—the grief and hope are ours.*

* This young gentleman fell a victim to the treachery of the Chinese,
at the close of the late war with China.

THE GOURD.

JONAH, chap. iv.

—o—

BENEATH a sweet and pleasant gourd,
　My watchless heart was sleeping;
But a worm came gnawing to its root,
　And turned my joy to weeping:
And, as it pale and sickly grew,
　And daily seemed declining,
My heart grew wan and sickly too,
　And sinfully repining.

" And, wilt thou, Lord,"—this was my cry—
　" Thus leave me all alone?
" Others have store of blessings, I
　" Have but this cherished one;

" One shadowing shelter on the waste.
  " T'assuage life's burning sky:
" Till these fierce heats be overpast,
  " O, spare it, lest I die."

Thus did my tortured spirit rave,
  Thus madly bit the dust:
In Him, who had the power to save,
  I put no filial trust.
Faithless, despairing at my fate,
  This plunged me into sin:
When Passion forces Reason's gate,
  Legions of foes rush in.

A voice!—" Presumptuous mortal know
  " Thy Sovereign, and be still!
" The plant is mine, to bid it grow,
  " Or wither at my will.
" 'Tis thine to lie, with humbler tone,
  " Submissive in the dust
" And whatsoe'er the event, to own
  " Thy punishment is just.

" Did I not form thee—hath the clay,
  "Thus to its Former spoke?
"The patient steer, the live-long day
  "Yields to its master's yoke:
"Angels beneath their trembling wings,
  "Before me veil their face.
"Then humbly bow, and learn to trust
  "The hand thou can'st not trace."

I heard that voice: I hear it still
  And bow to its control,
Yet gently did its influence fill
  Each chamber of my soul.
Though wounded, not despairing, now
  I own the hand of God,
Chastised, yet not forsaken, bow ;
  For Mercy wields the rod.

THISTLE-DOWN.

" Cursed is the ground for thy sake."————" Thorns also and thistles
shall it bring forth to thee."—GENESIS iii. 17, 18.

—o—

AH! go ye sad remembrancers,
　　Obedient to your Lord,
And scatter down to future years,
　　The signets of His word.

If whirled upon the stormy West,
　　Or sailing with the breeze,
Or, scarce afloat on eve's calm breast,
　　Still speaking His decrees.

Hover round Infidelity,
    Wave thee before her eyes,
Press her to own, fulfilled in thee,
    The message of the skies.

Winged by the curse, spread want around,
    Preach vengeance as ye fly,
Then bid the troubled thought rebound
    To peaceful Calvary.

Aloud denounce the righteous woe,
    On Eden's exiles laid:
But louder yet, where'er ye go,
    Proclaim the ransom paid.

Bosom'd in down, lo! curses rove,
    On silent pinions borne:
Our least suspected comforts prove
    The parents of a thorn.

Great condescending Husbandman,
　　Behold the lurking seed,
And grant, O grant Thy saving hand
　　To crush the deathful weed.

This Poem is found amongst Mr. Pell's manuscripts, and is inserted for
its merit—but it is attributed by him to Thomas Rogers.

BURTON, PRINTER, GREAT YARMOUTH.

www.ingramcontent.com/pod-product-compliance
Lightning Source LLC
Chambersburg PA
CBHW030006030726
47499CB00008B/2920